Habitat Hints

BRIDGE

Written by Brenda Scott Royce

Illustrated by Joseph Wilkins

JOLLY
FiSH
PRESS
Mendota Heights, Minnesota

Book design by Sarah Taplin
Illustrations by Joseph Wilkins (Beehive Illustration)

Published in the United States by Jolly Fish Press, an imprint of North Star Editions, Inc.

First Edition
First Printing, 2022

This is a work of fiction. Names, characters, places, and incidents are either the product of the author's imagination or are used fictitiously, and any resemblance to actual persons living or dead, business establishments, events, or locales is entirely coincidental.

Library of Congress Cataloging-in-Publication Data (pending)
978-1-63163-628-8 (paperback)
978-1-63163-627-1 (hardcover)

Jolly Fish Press
North Star Editions, Inc.
2297 Waters Drive
Mendota Heights, MN 55120
www.jollyfishpress.com

Printed in the United States of America

TABLE OF CONTENTS

CHAPTER 1

New Exhibit

Beep, beep, beep.

A construction vehicle backed up at Mountain Bluff Zoo. The sound could be heard throughout the zoo. Katy Nichols and Micah Draper watched the machine. Its backhoe moved into position. Then it dumped a mound of dirt into the middle of an empty exhibit. It was Saturday morning. The Junior Volunteers had just arrived at the zoo. Micah and Katy were standing alongside Corinna, Katy's mother. Corinna worked at the zoo as an animal keeper.

"It's fun to watch the new exhibit being built," Corinna said. "But I have hungry animals to feed." She waved at a man walking over. "Here comes Sam. You two will be working with him today."

Sam was a tall, sturdy-looking man. He reminded Katy of a bear. Sam was wearing a keeper's uniform and an orange hard hat. Corinna introduced

him to the kids. Then she headed toward the koala habitat.

"Thanks for helping me out today," Sam told the kids. "We have lots to do. We have to get this habitat ready for . . ." Sam trailed off.

"For *who*?" Micah prodded.

"Yes, please tell us," Katy added. "What kind of animal is going to live here?"

"I could tell you," Sam said. A smile formed on his face. "But I have a better idea. Let's see if you can figure it out."

CHAPTER 2

Guessing Game

"Figure it out?" Katy asked. "How?"

"Look for clues." Sam motioned around him. "Have you noticed that no two zoo habitats are the same? Each one meets the needs of the animals that live in it. Would you put a giraffe in an enclosure that was built for a turtle?"

Micah giggled. "Probably not."

"When we design a habitat, we start

with research," Sam said. "Does the animal fly? Does it swim, climb, or burrow underground? Does it need room to run or places to hide?"

"That's a lot of questions," Katy said. She pulled out her notebook.

"After we learn all about the animals, we start thinking about the habitat," Sam said. "Should we include trees, water, sand, or rocks? What about a fence or a moat? And that's just the beginning."

Sam led the kids to the back of the new exhibit. There, workers were unloading supplies. "You'll be helping get the habitat ready. As you do, think about its features. Think about what kinds of animals might live here. If you guess correctly, I'll let you two cut the ribbon at the opening ceremony."

Katy and Micah traded glances. They were excited. Then Micah said, "I think the animal is—"

"Wait," Sam said. "You only get one guess. So, gather all the information you can. Then make your decision."

"Okay," Katy said. "We will."

"Great!" Sam said. "Now let's get to work." He handed them each a paintbrush. He pointed at the fence around the habitat. "You can start by helping me paint this fence."

CHAPTER 3

Zoo Clues

Katy and Micah worked carefully. They put a thick coat of brown paint on the fence. Micah paused now and then. He snapped photos of the construction in progress.

Katy finished one part of the fence. She set down her paintbrush. Then she picked up her notebook. "I'll start a list of clues," she said to Micah. "The habitat is very large. There are a couple of trees. They could be for climbing, or maybe just for shade."

"There's a strong wooden fence," Micah said. "But the habitat is not screened in. And there's no roof. A bird could just fly away."

"Not all birds can fly," Katy said as she scribbled notes. "But you're right. It doesn't look like an aviary. What else?"

Micah shrugged. "One side is flat and grassy."

"The other side looks like a giant crater," Katy noted.

"Maybe it's a skate park!" Micah held out both hands at his sides. He pretended he was skateboarding.

"It's not a skate park, silly. It might be a pool."

Just then, a worker rolled out a thick hose. The worker began filling the pool with water.

Micah sighed. "I guess that makes more sense than a skate park."

After a while, they finished painting the fence. Then the kids helped the gardener. They watered the plants in the habitat. As they did so, they continued their detective work. "It must be a large animal that spends time both on land and in the water," Katy said.

Micah's eyes lit up. "I know what it is. An alligator!"

Katy looked thoughtfully around the habitat. The pool was surrounded by sand and tall plants. It reminded her of a beach. She could picture an alligator swimming in the pool. And she could see it climbing out. The alligator might sun itself on the sand. It could also hide among the plants. She smiled at Micah. "I think you're right."

"We only get one guess," he said. "Are we sure?"

Katy nodded. "Let's go tell Sam."

CHAPTER 4

What Eats Hay?

Micah and Katy walked around to the back of the habitat. They knocked on a door marked "STAFF ONLY." They called out for Sam. Another keeper told them that Sam was picking up more supplies. But he would return soon.

"I hope so." Micah was bouncing on the balls of his feet. "We have something important to tell him."

The keeper held up a walkie-talkie. "I'll let him know."

As they waited, a man in a pickup truck pulled up nearby. The driver hopped out of the truck. He was holding a clipboard. "Is Sam here? I'm looking for him," he told the kids.

"So are we," Katy said. "He'll be right back."

"Great. I'll start unloading." The driver removed a cart from his truck. Then he walked around to the back of the vehicle. The bed of the pickup was loaded with stacks of hay bales.

"That's a lot of hay," Micah said. "Do you live on a farm?"

"No," the driver said. He chuckled. Then he began moving hay onto the cart. "I work at the zoo commissary. That's where all the food is prepared for the animals. Everything comes into the commissary. Then I deliver the food all around the zoo."

Micah looked at the bales for a second. Then he pulled Katy aside. He whispered into her ear. "Do alligators eat hay?"

"I don't think so," she said glumly.

Sam returned moments later. He showed the driver where to put the hay. Then he turned to the kids. "I hear you have something to tell me. Have you figured it out?"

Micah and Katy looked at each other and frowned. "No," Micah said.

"We thought we did," Katy said. "But we need to do more research. We'll have the answer tomorrow."

CHAPTER 5

Opening Ceremony

When Katy's mom pulled up outside Micah's house the next morning, Micah was already waiting. He waved goodbye to his father. Then climbed in the back seat of Katy's car. "I did lots of research last night," he told her.

"Me too." She opened her notebook and began reading. "The habitat is huge, so it must be a big animal. It spends time in the water and on land.

It eats hay. I'm thinking it could be an elephant or a hippopotamus."

Micah nodded. "That's what I think, too!"

"But which is it?" Katy asked. "We only get one guess."

Micah sighed. "Hippos and elephants are both large, social animals. They both like to swim. But hippos spend more time in the water."

"You're right," Katy said. "I read that hippos spend up to sixteen hours a day in the water."

"You said the empty pool looked like a giant crater," Micah said. "That's really big. So it must be super important to the animal that's going to live there."

"Good point," Katy said. "Plus, the other side of the habitat is flat and grassy. It reminds me of a big lawn. I read that hippos are grazers. They eat lots of grass."

By the time they arrived at the zoo, Katy and Micah had made up their minds. They hurried to the new habitat and found Sam. Before the keeper could even say "good morning," they shouted, "It's a hippo!"

"You're right," Sam said. He gave them each a high five. "Actually, it's *two* hippos!"

The next Saturday, Katy and Micah stood in front of the hippopotamus habitat. They were with Sam and other members of the zoo crew. A thick yellow ribbon had been strung across the pathway leading to the habitat. A large crowd had gathered. There were all there for the exhibit's opening ceremony.

The zoo's director thanked everyone for coming. Then she handed a large pair of scissors to Sam. "Sam Kipling helped plan this habitat," the director

said. "And he will be taking care of the hippos. So, he will cut the ribbon."

Sam stepped forward. "Actually, I made a promise to my two Junior Volunteers. I said that they could have the honors. Micah Draper and Katy Nichols?" He gave the kids the oversized scissors. Together, they cut the ribbon. People cheered and made their way down the pathway.

Katy and Micah watched as the guests saw the hippos for the first time. The hippos were a mother and daughter named Rosie and Tess.

Rosie was soaking in the pool. Only her eyes and ears were above water. Tess bobbed up and down nearby. She pushed a big plastic ball with her snout.

Micah pointed at the pair and smiled. "They sure like their pool."

Katy nodded. "It was so much fun gathering clues and learning about animal habitats. I wonder what our next assignment will be?"

THINK ABOUT IT

 Sam says that no two zoo habitats are alike. What are some reasons why a habitat for a giraffe would be wrong for a turtle?

 There are many different jobs in the zoo. In this story, Katy and Micah meet animal keepers, a gardener, a delivery person, and the zoo director. Can you think of other jobs people do at the zoo?

Pretend you are designing a zoo habitat for your favorite animal. What would you include? Draw the habitat or make a model using a shoebox and craft supplies.

ABOUT THE AUTHOR

Brenda Scott Royce is the author of more than twenty books for adults and children. Animals are her favorite subject to write about. She has worked as a chimpanzee keeper at an animal sanctuary and traveled on wildlife expeditions to Africa and South America. In her free time, she helps injured birds as a volunteer with SoCal Parrot Rescue.

ABOUT THE ILLUSTRATOR

Joseph Wilkins is an illustrator living and working in the seaside town of Brighton, England. A graduate of Falmouth College of Arts in Cornwall, Joseph has spent the last fifteen years forging a successful freelance career. When not drawing, he can be found messing around with bicycles or on the beach with his family.

DOGGIE DAYCARE
IS OPEN FOR BUSINESS!

Join siblings Shawn and Kat Choi as they start their own pet-sitting service out of their San Francisco home. Every dog they meet has its own special personality, sending the kids on fun (and furry) adventures all over the city!

"Shawn and Kat are supported by a diverse cast in which readers of many colors can see themselves reflected. Problem-solvers and dog lovers alike will pounce on this series." —Kirkus Reviews